# Tweedy
## The Clown Who Lost His Nose

Written by
**Tweedy the Clown**

Illustrated by
**Daniel Duncan**

Tweedy is a clown.

He wears colorful socks,
very long shoes, and best of all,
a bright red nose.

Tweedy loves to make people laugh
when he is in the circus ring.

Tweedy also has a pet, a mop named Steev!

Steev is always nearby. Can you see him?

Whenever Tweedy gets ready for a show,
he always puts on his bright red nose first.
Tweedy knows his red clown nose is
what makes people laugh the most.

Tweedy had the audience crying with laughter!

But today, he couldn't find it! Tweedy looked everywhere in his dressing room, but his red clown nose was nowhere to be found.

But before the ringmaster could answer, Tweedy thought he saw his round red nose. He grabbed it, but...oops!

It wasn't his clown nose at all...

Tweedy grabbed the curtain to hide behind it, but...oops!

The curtain pole crashed down, landing on the ringmaster and knocking his hat off. Some children started to laugh, but Tweedy didn't notice.

But before she could answer, Tweedy
thought he saw his round red nose.
He grabbed it, but...oops!
It wasn't his clown nose at all...

...it was a bright red bolt holding the heavy weights on the bar.

But before the juggler could answer, Tweedy thought he saw his round red nose. He grabbed it, but...oops! It wasn't his clown nose at all...

CRASH!

All the children and most of the grown-ups were laughing now, but Tweedy still didn't notice.

A big shiny motorcycle roared into the ring and up to the top of a huge ramp. The rider was about to perform an amazing stunt when Tweedy shouted to him.

I've lost my nose! Nobody will laugh if I'm not wearing my bright red nose. Have you seen it?

But before the rider could answer, Tweedy thought he saw his round red nose. He ran up the ladder and grabbed it, but...oops! It wasn't his clown nose at all...

Tweedy slid out of the barrel with a slosh and a plop. He sat there in his pink patterned pants, soaking wet.

He still hadn't found his bright red nose.

The rest of the circus performers gathered around.
"Oh no," thought Tweedy.
"I've messed up their show..."

HA HA HA!

HOORAY FOR TWEEDY!

HO HO!

HA!

HA HA HA!

HA HA HA! HOORAY FOR TWEEDY!

## ABOUT THE AUTHOR

When Tweedy left school he joined a circus. He fell in love with clowning and has been a clown ever since. He's accomplished in most circus skills, can play many musical instruments, and can perform magic tricks. He clowns in theaters, on TV and in film, but is best known as being the clown at Giffords Circus in the UK.

In 2023 Tweedy was awarded the British Empire Medal in King Charles III's very first New Year Honours list.

## ABOUT THE ILLUSTRATOR

Daniel grew up on the outskirts of London, playing soccer outside when it wasn't raining, and drawing the rest of the time.

He studied illustration at university, and has worked as a children's illustrator ever since. Daniel now works from his home studio in Amersham, in the UK, where he lives with his wife, two young daughters, and Siamese cat Diego.

THIS BOOK IS DEDICATED TO SHARON, WILLOW, ANN, AND JACK

**Written by** Tweedy the Clown
**Illustrated by** Daniel Duncan

**Editor** Francesca Harper
**Additional Editorial** Lisa Davis, Penny Morris
**US Senior Editor** Shannon Beatty
**Senior Art Editor** Charlotte Bull
**Senior Production Editor** Nikoleta Parasaki
**Senior Production Controller** Inderjit Bhullar
**Publisher** Francesca Young
**Art Director** Mabel Chan
**Publishing Director** Sarah Larter

First American Edition, 2025
Published in the United States by DK Publishing,
a division of Penguin Random House LLC
1745 Broadway, 20th Floor, New York, NY 10019

Artwork Copyright © Daniel Duncan, 2025
Tweedy Author Photo Copyright © Paul Reid, 2025
Layout and Design Copyright © 2025
Dorling Kindersley Limited
25 26 27 28 29 10 9 8 7 6 5 4 3 2 1
001–340345–Feb/2025

All rights reserved.
Without limiting the rights under the copyright reserved above, no part of this publication may be reproduced, stored in or introduced into a retrieval system, or transmitted, in any form, or by any means (electronic, mechanical, photocopying, recording, or otherwise), without the prior written permission of the copyright owner.
Published in Great Britain by
Dorling Kindersley Limited

A catalog record for this book
is available from the Library of Congress.
ISBN 978-0-5938-5040-4

DK books are available at special discounts when purchased in bulk for sales promotions, premiums, fund-raising, or educational use. For details, contact: DK Publishing Special Markets, 1745 Broadway, 20th Floor, New York, NY 10019
SpecialSales@dk.com

Printed and bound in China

www.dk.com

This book was made with Forest Stewardship Council™ certified paper – one small step in DK's commitment to a sustainable future.
Learn more at www.dk.com/uk/information/sustainability